I0580554

DOUGLAS C. GRANUM

JUDITH'S GAP

Chapter 1

To me, she means nothing! She means nothing to me anymore. Is that plain enough for you? I've said it two ways, same meaning.

These things, these gut-changing life events, well you can probably hear the shaky emotion in my voice. Actually, the corners of my mouth pull down when I even mention her name. Do I care? Yes, I care. However, I want her out of my soul, out of my bones, out of my thoughts.

I am saying this as unadorned, as humanly, as possible through the sad, static wretchedness of our time together. There was a time, a few moments, when our lives were my dream. She was grand. I'm saying it: Once there was a time when she meant everything to me.

What is it about hopeless love? It's so exciting on one hand and so freighted with disappointment. Sort of a dumpster dive, and that one time, only one time, you find a gem.

What I mean- well I guess I would ask- do you realize what I mean by that? That once in a while you win, and the object of your desire also finds you fascinating. So it was like this then.

I would have given her my existence on Earth. You see, here I am saying she should live and I should die, that's how crazy I was for her. Lay down my life, take a round to protect her, hell yes.

With her it was full frontal assault. It took what it took. I would have taken whatever it took. You go to war with the army you have. Love was a blood sport, it was war with her.

God, life is so, but look now. No, she is not exciting, her excitement, for me, has left the station. To me, well she doesn't stir me anymore. Not remotely. A roadkill, really. Not even that. I don't- I mean, well, what I am trying to say is (don't laugh, since I am taking about her here again), but, well anyway, laugh or not, I try not to think of her.

She taught me so much I never wanted to know. Never did I want ash trays thrown at me, angry food fights, to listen to her rancor, her petty spite, her mistreatment of our friends and even people we didn't know.

"Fuck love and the horse it rode in on!" she would screech. How do you guard yourself against that? I will tell you this, that type of malevolence is not easily pried from my thoughts. I don't wish her harm. However, I want to forget Judith today and forever.

She is in the arms of others now. Good luck to them. Her, him, whatever. How can I pry her love-hate from my soul, my in-testines? She intensifies. Sometimes, when I awake in sweaty turmoil late at night, I, despite my resistance, remember her, even though I don't want to. She prowls my dreaming, fleeing self through chambered dark caves in my nightmares. My thoughts drift at those times when I am half asleep, unguarded. Then, snap your fingers, and just like that, out of a deep sleep, I am sud-denly, in a nanosecond, glaringly awake. Awake, my first thought is her. I lie there thinking about a lot of things, mostly how we were in good times. You've been there. First one side, then the other, knees pulled up, on my back with my hands behind my head. After a while my shoulders hurt. I roll on my other side, same thing. Adjust the pillow, place my legs and arms and hand, then, that last thing to adjust, my mind.

In that nightmarish moment I hear her torn, grating voice yelling, her heaviness creeping over the top of my pillow, smelling like a damp green miasma.

It seems so strange, thinking of her now. Despite my obvious confusion there were those moments when I couldn't breathe when I thought of her. She caught my breath, strangled my consciousness to the exclusion of all other thought.

Have you ever been so in love that the first thought in the morning was her? The last thoughts as you drifted off to sleep were of her lips? How could I say enough about her lips? I can say they were sculptural, sexual and full. When she was aroused and kissing me it was with engorged Watusi-like slaps.

Her eyes were the color of very pale

martini ice in vodka. Her iris on her right eye had a darker blue slash of color that went from the white of her eye into her pupil. Her smile was expansive and somewhat masculine. Breasts, like her lips, engorged and luscious. She had an aristocratic bearing. She floated when she walked.

Look, I know I am talking about her physical self, but her moves coupled with her intelligence was really incredible to me.

Somedays it seemed like we were only together to use each other up.

One of the first times we made love, or more accurately, had sex, was in a little cramped gray worn shingled logger's hotel in Astoria, Oregon. The King Hotel was named after the great king salmon runs that the Columbia River is famous for.

Its flashing neon sign out front was on the river road that ran along the Columbia River through Astoria and on down the coast to California. The sign only said

"King", the "Hotel" part of the neon was burned out. The "King" part of the sign sizzled and spat. The tawdry King Hotel itself was part of the same old decaying building that the Union Logger Bar was in. It faced the Columbia River in back of the Union Loggers Bar. The bar dominated the street front.

The actual hotel had no identifying signs left burning out on the street as the hotel neon, as stated, was burned out. Someone once said, "An ugly building can make a beautiful ruin." Not the King Hotel. It was a ruin, and obviously would never be beautiful. It never was.

We had driven north up Highway 101 through salty sand dunes, covered and studded with stunted pines, small coastal farms, and villages. The first bar we came to after passing over the Astoria Bridge was the Union Logger. We parked on the street, kissed longingly in the car, then while holding hands we rushed across the busy road through heavy rain. The fog, normal for the lower Columbia, had yet to set in.

I pushed open the squeaking swinging door for Judith. We both stepped over the door sill into the smoky decaying tavern. We were hit in the face with the stink of deodorant, cigarette smoke, cedar, and booze. The visuals were National Geographic 1937, black and white. There was an antique Wurlitzer juke box. This instrument was lit up like a carousel. It glowed, pulsating pastels, pale pink, light green, sea foam blue, and on, one electric glowing color chasing another color over its plastic face.

As we walked into the cavernous room, an old slouchy kind of man standing in front of the Wurlitzer juke box dropped in two quarters, and out came "Waltz Across Texas" by Ernest Tubb.

Back once again to the middle of the room, the slovenly looking old man slipped his arm around his partner, and they took off in some strange drunken waltz. Two beat, tired looking people, apparently holding each other up, were in some alcohol induced trance/dance.

The man may be a logger, his partner a tired looking cannery worker, maybe an Indian woman still in her white fish smeared pants. The smears had now dried.

Except for the sodden couple on the dance floor, the place was empty. The cigarette smoke drifted like distant galaxies in the high-ceilinged room. Ernest Tubb's voice bounced around the empty room, echoing off the walls.

"Like a story book ending I'm lost in your charms, I could waltz across Texas with you." Ernest Tubb's voice, always kind of deep and old timey and flat, was perfect for the Union Loggers Bar.

High on one wall was a painting of Mt. Hood, faded by generations of tobacco smoke and smoke from the grill.

Generations of respirating fishermen and fisherwomen, panting and struggling in grotesque embrace, clutching and grabbing at each other while dancing. This little pantomime of caring was really the face of raw sex. Little rooms upstairs awaited.

All of the rotating dancers circled the floor. The front windows steamed over, heavy breathing and sweating and bleeding, spit and sneezing, lower Columbia cough and the Spanish flu.

Wrapped in each other's arms, dancing to old Finnish songs, or Norwegian songs, or Scottish jigs.

These grey walls had seen it all.

Play sucky under the table? The floors under these tables had knee marks.

One night a young Finnish beauty with chrome blonde hair walked into the bar and placed an empty milk bottle on the bar. She bet $10 each to anyone who would bet that she could stand on the bar over the bottle and piss into it and not spill a drop.

Judith grabbed me and whirled me around a couple of times, laughing, raising her feet high like in a clog dance. Her dress rode up her thigh halfway, she looked splendid. Her nine-inch spikes were red.

Walking over to the bar we sat down on the worn maroon vinyl bar stools. Don't ask. Anyway, I put my hand palm up under Judith just as she sat down. She screamed that loud little high E Southern Belle squeal that she probably learned from her French Louisiana Indian mother. The old waitress took another drag on her weed, coughed, looked at us smiling and said,

"Well now ain't ya the pair."

Judith grabbed me by the front of my shirt and kissed me hard on the lips.

Spinning around after sitting down we faced a dusty backbar filled with a seemingly endless assortment of bottles. All of them, to some degree, part empty or part full, depending on how you see your world.

Our waitress, a tired, complacent looking old woman talking into her cell phone said,

"Hold on a moment darlin'. No, God damn it Ole, stop that shit."

Then turning toward us, smiling a toothless smile, asking us what we wanted, she coughed. We didn't ask her any hard questions. Judith just pantomimed to the sausages, then two fingers to her throat, then held up her fist with her thumb for a spout and two fingers for two dark beers. Judith then pointed to the tired old waitresses' phone and indicated that we didn't want to interrupt.

She nodded, laying down her phone, gave us a couple of beers, plastic forks, and napkins. Help yourselves, bon appétit, she gestured with her hand with the missing index finger, with the smoking cigarette still in it.

We both had a cold greasy sausage from a gallon jar on the bar, chased by a dark Guinness beer for our late breakfast. Judith looked at the tired old gal and pointed to the bar. Go ahead Honey, go ahead, she gestured for Judith to go ahead, help ourselves, get us whatever we wanted. Judith got us a slice of cold pizza, a large pickle, some pigs feet, some trail mix in a shallow red and white checked bowl, popcorn, salted bar nuts, and a couple more Guinness.

We munched and chewed and flirted, drank sometimes, spinning all the way around on the stool to stop and kiss. She was wearing one of her thin silk dresses, which, when I slid my hand up beneath her silk dress, there was only Judith all the way.

She had on a white turtleneck over the silk dress which was over a cream-colored bra.

For the hell of it, we bet on some pull

tabs and punch boards, and God damn it if we didn't win 100 bucks. Feeling lucky, we tried again for the next thirty minutes, and managed to lose $50. Beer in hand, we wandered around the room looking at the old photographs of the early days of fishing on the lower Columbia sand bars. Fishing was done by gill net using horses, while out in the deeper channels fishing was done with small classic gill net boats.

There were fading pictures of loggers standing on enormous fallen trees with long, two man crosscut saws at their sides.

There were other photographs of women dressed with white beanie hats with white rubber aprons. They were gutting and cleaning long troughs of silver salmon. The pictures had all faded, and the glass covering the photographs had turned yellow from decades of cigarette smoke. Across one photograph someone had wiped their finger.

We settled back down at the scarred bar playing chess and checkers. We started drinking and eating, which debauched into a drunken long afternoon. Our tired old gal, our waitress, made us hamburgers and really pretty good French fries.

She pulled up a stool on her side of the bar and sat talking with us. She told us she lost her front teeth trying to break up a fight between two women, each with a bottle, here two years ago. Then she told us a truck had crashed through the front door and killed one of her regulars, who used to sit at his favorite table by the window. She pointed out a tiny scar that was still visible in the window casing. Then she said,

"Time robs us of all, even memory. I can remember being a little girl helping my dad on his gill netter when I was 10, but what the hell, I can't remember what I had for breakfast!" and laughed, followed by a chronic smoker's cough. Just then the door swung open and a couple walked in. She got up and left us.

Looking out the open door for that moment I saw that the rain had ceased, and fog was starting to fill in the houses across the street.

Walking over to the pool table we played pool, setting our single shot glasses of Stolichnaya vodka, which we had switched to after the beers, on the side of the pool table. I have never been good at pool, but then neither was Judith. Pool, vodka, pool, vodka. No winners, no losers.

Next, we shot darts, ate pickled pig's feet, elk jerky, chips and salsa, had hot cheese-melt sandwiches, and more Stoli. The more she drank the more fun we had. She was great sometimes. At other times when she drank she became ugly in spirit, morose and dark.

I drank enough until, while weaving to the toilet, the old antique photos of long dead fisherman and their fish boats swam, rolled and listed, as though they were actually at sea and not on the halls and walls of a cheap, dingy, crummy riverside hotel.

I stumbled through the green door that read "Gents" with a cutout of a commercial fisherman tacked on it. Sizing up the urinal to pee, I stumbled and crashed my head against the pale green graffiti-covered wall above the galvanized can.

Standing there peeing I looked idly at the graffiti.

"Why look up here, the joke's in your hand"

"Lizzy does it deeper"

"Sally is home alone tonight. PLEASE, please, please, call 503-673-1213"

"Billy has it in his pants just for you"

The graffiti undulated in my blurry vision under the single bare bulb in the center of the ceiling. The toilet, far back in the gloom in its thin green plywood enclosure, was in near total darkness. I could make out half of a toilet paper roll hanging on the wall.

Slouching there, my sodden head against the wall, I looked straight down at the cigarette butts, a purple piece of chewing gum, and a single black condom that glowed in the dark in the bottom of the orange rusted galvanized urinal.

As I tried to adjust my drunken piss dance, I aimed for the wavering small red rubber target filter in the center of the urinal, while attempting to miss my shoes.

No surprise, no hand towels, so washing my hands in cold water, I dried them on my jeans.

As I came out of the swinging door of the toilet, I saw Judith standing at the rain splashed dirty window at the front of the bar overlooking the now foggy street. Metal halide lamps across the street outline her hair and her figure. She had a dirty yellow halo. On the window was a neon sign advertising Four Sixes beer.

She turned just as I walked out of the lime green toilet, shouting across the room to the tattooed old bar maid, asking,

"Is there a hotel around here?"

The old barmaid took a cigarette out of her mouth between her index and middle finger, which had the first two joints missing, and put her hand up to her ear, looking at Judith. Judith yelled,

"Hotel?"

The barmaid, pointing with her hand with the cigarette still between her fingers to a small black and white sign just over the toilet doors. The sign had one of those pointing index finger hands pointing to a message. "Rooms for rent by the hour or longer. See the bar keeper for more information. Food allowed. No pets. Includes electric hotplate."

The room was on the second floor, up

worn creaking wooden stairs. The stairwell was freezing, a window being broken at the end of the hall.

The wooden stairs were trashed by decades of logger's boots with corks. Corks, if you don't know, are a series of smallish spikes on the soles of logging boots for traction when walking on wet muddy fallen timber.

The key to room 7 was the old-fashioned kind. When I opened the door the overwhelming smell of bleach and deodorant assailed my nose with caustic corrosion. It felt to be about 85 degrees in the close little room.

It appeared that no one had been in that room for a long time. The air was flat and dead. The bed, with a grey woolen blanket on it, sagged dramatically in the middle as though it might touch the floor.

I went to the old double-hung single pane window, the only one in the room, and pulled it up and open with both hands to air out the hot stagnant room. A radiator clicked-snapped under the window, giving off waves of heat.

A seagull sitting on the windowsill flew off when I opened the window, crying raucously.

Leaning out the open window I could look right down into the muddy Columbia River, that part of the hotel being on piers over the river. I spit and watched as my spit spiraled, then flatten out through the moist air, finally landing as a small white frothy blob far down in the Columbia. The white glob of spit, when it hit the water, was instantly carried off and down river. There was a rainbow oil slick.

I turned back to the heated room. Judith was in the bathroom with the door closed.

I sat down thoughtlessly on the bed, heavily impaired by the Stoli, and slipped right off onto the floor. I climbed drunkenly back up onto my knees on the worn linoleum floor, and then back up onto the bed, with a little bit more caution this time. I blankly stared out the window at the great Astoria steel bridge which connects Oregon and Washington state. The bridge was covered with flocks of seagulls and cormorants.

Judith came out of the bathroom where I could hear the toilet still running. She had taken off her coat and her white sweater, leaving her green patterned dress on. She stood in the doorway to the bathroom with the little yellow light behind her, naked from her waist up.

I looked at her in that light and wondered how it was that some women with the most beautiful faces can have such failures of bodies, and then there are the women with the bodies of Venus and the faces of a thumb.

And then you had Judith, who had it all, except somewhere in all that beauty lied

the careless attitude that she was so strik-
ing that she could be and do as she pleased
with anyone. She was the hood ornament.

She came and climbed on top of me, sitting astride my lap. As she walked to the
bed I thought of a remark from a friend of
mine who said,

"I could never be married to a woman
who I don't find beautiful."

She leaned over me, her hair brushing
my face. I could smell her expensive perfume. She kissed me, a great sloppy Watusi
kiss, winked leeringly, then pulled off my
hat and threw it across the room. She then
kicked off her red high heel spikes.

Next, she pulled my sweater over my
head, then peeled my black t-shirt up and
off. Sliding off my lap, she dropped to her
knees while undoing my belt buckle. Next,
while leaning her lips into my crotch, she
blew her heated, alcohol-soaked breath
through my zipped-up zipper. I could feel

her hot breath through the zipper. It made me stir, and then some.

Sliding back up she looked at me, winked, kissed me again, then slid down, and this time she unzipped and opened my blue jeans. She pulled off my shoes and socks, then tugging and jerking she pulled off my pants. She looked up into my face again and winked and kissed my knee. She got up, leaving me lying on the bed, and went over to the coffee table, throwing the Bible and ash tray onto the couch. She then turned and, reaching into my boxers, grabbed my erection, pulling me up and leading me to the side of the little coffee table. Pulling off my bulging boxer shorts, she bid me lie down naked on my back on the small cool table. I lay there for all the world like some fleshy sun dial. She peeled off all her cloths. Then while straddling me, with both of her feet on each side of me, me on my back on the cool little coffee table, she settled with my erectness deep inside her drunken heat.

In those days I never knew what to expect.

Surprise!

Those days are the same as these days, I still don't know what to expect.

A soul in torment, hoping always for her heat, her warmth, rarely finding solace. That was me.

Cold as ice. Remember the line from the song, "You're as cold as ice. You're willing to sacrifice our love."? What a joke.

Love? No, no love. Physical sex, yes. Spiritual love, no.

How many people does it take to carry the love load in a relationship? Can only one person be "in love" while the other only likes the other a lot? Is it semantics, this poetic love, or is it really food?

Is sex food? That nourishing early dawn at the luscious, rounded breast of your mother. The milk so warm, so vital, so sensual. Can a nourishing mother not love her child that she is nourishing?

Or is it that love is never equal? That one or the other loves more or less?

Perhaps some have vastly different ideas of what love means. Love, what is that really?

I actually started to listen to love songs with some kind of abstract hope that what I saw in Judith and felt clutching at my being wasn't what I saw. It was nowhere near to what I hoped for.

This was unlike me, not to just say, "Screw it." I remembered dates, days, moments out of time that we spent together. She gave me a little gift, and I remembered the date and even the hour. I never did that before in my whole life. Why now?

But then you know, don't you? I always hoped she would be different. She never was. I always thought I could change her. I never could.

It's always so simple if we just allow the game to come to us, but no. We go muddying the water, charging ahead until visibility is gone. Then we ask ourselves, "What the hell?"

Cast into the stream before you walk in if you would get the first trout.

To be first with her, however, was a daunting task. Hot potato.

She kindled the lure of love in me. I stopped being as she ran her hands over me. I was stilled. What's next?

Judith knew my spots of love and passion. My entire body was a plainly read roadmap of my sensual vulnerabilities for her.

Where are you most wide open to the lugubriously archway leading to your fervor and ardor which so often ends in failure?

Which parts of our ardor lie on the cut-ting room floor?

What are the chances from the beginning of time that you are here? You are at the tip of existence.

Is there a song "Impossible Song"? If not, there should be.

You can see here I am thinking of her once more when I continually tell myself I won't. Have you ever been addicted? You tell yourself you won't, but you do. You continue with the addiction until you break the chain.

I still dream about her at night. Drunk on love, willing, forcing myself not to see her lack of love for me. That about sums it up.

I know it has been said ad infinitum, love is blind. I was blinded by her. I was that tawny deer staring at the headlights, wondering what that blinding light was as I became a roadkill, with a round between the eyes.

Look, I just want to forget, I'm trying to forget. I don't even know why I am telling you this. What's the saying? Love is so short, forgetting so long.

Forgetting is a whole hell of a lot easier said than done for me. Forgetting is a long time.

How can you forget what you once said was part of your blood, bones, even your bone marrow?

Love is a brutal blood sport.

I did love her. You should know that by now, if you know nothing else, I did. I craved her, desired her, wanted to protect her, feed her, feed myself from her Venus de Willendorf body.

I was seized up like a rusted steel nut by my own terminal enchantment for this witchy Goddess.

Who cast the spell? We know who loves whom! We also know who can't love, and who won't have a sweet little pink baby at her proud breast.

Have you ever noticed that every little ditty on the radio, the television, the movies, books, and on and on ad infinitum, it's all about love and baby, baby, baby I love you?

It is fortunate for mankind that we are all on a circular wheel. We are born, live, die. We can forget, one of man's big blessings. We can ignore. Along comes the next generation and the next, each making gains and failures, and nowhere so obvious as in the personal love between two people. Like the reactive divers' chemical elements that we are, if two people react and change in love, they are changed forever.

Love is a rampaging emotion that is at its most virulent when you are in the spring of your love.

Try as you will, you somehow buy into that brown nutty crap and inexorably we do change, like it or not.

With her I made myself believe it, believe it until that last day when I wrote her name with a piece of twisted grey driftwood on a distant saltwater beach. She, my Goddess no more.

Love makes the world turn. I want an unclouded world when I am in love. In those days, she played me like a cheap guitar. Always sort of out of tune, like a Chinese orchestra.

The guitar strings 3/8 of an inch from the fret board, always straining. The music sounded strained, our "love" discordant.

For me it was turbulent and murky, like walking in the dark. I hate stubbing my toes. When you are the instrument and not the musician you don't have a lot to say about the music.

When I met her, I walked under her overcast world, something that rarely changed. She almost never ventured into mine, except to take what she wanted of me.

I was her pawn, her mark, her lackey, and I loved it, until I didn't. Falling out of love isn't that easy until it gets a hold of your twisted cerebellum, and then you get a clearer picture. One gets to thinking some way it might be possible to fall out of love, but that reasoning only comes later.

I'm thinking you will know what I mean here.

If what I am describing here hasn't happened to you, then you must be some paranormal, or lucky, and we know luck's a chance.

Does 50/50 exist in love? I sure as hell wouldn't put money on it. 50/50 always seems more to me like 40/60 against. I don't mind 40/60, I just want an even chance and a level playing field.

Being in love is to forget to guard your-self, but then you don't want to guard your-self when you are in love. What's that but contrived if you rigidly guard yourself?

However, each time you fall in love and it hurts, well, if you are normal, you become more guarded, don't you? How guarded must you be, how protected? Depends on the relationship, and with Judith I took what I could get.

Can you be madly, wildly in love and walk to it on your heels? I choose to run to it on my toes. Maybe you can go backwards, forwards, forwards and backwards at once, but I can't. Either I am in love or I'm not.

A short story may explain my view on love. Why I refused a request from a dear old friend when we were traveling in Spain where he knew many cultured and talented Spaniards. I called my friend the maître d'Madrid.

He knew the Bourbons, the Lugos, the Hernani family. Old families with ties to the founders of España. He was light on his feet, of a quick mind, and the royals loved him, mostly for his irreverence. His full beard and regal mustache, his clever bon mots, his charm, grace, and good looks. A man of the world, who spoke seven languages and wrote poetry in most of them.

One night after dining ferociously in the Bodega Urbana, I was praising the meal as sublime. I looked at him for a similar reply. He held his hand up with the smoking cigar between his index finger and his middle finger and said,

"One thing was missing. Yes, definitely missing from our meal."

I loved, even treasured our meal, like some meals I am sure you remember in your own life. What, I thought, was the something missing here?

The tablecloths were white pressed Egyptian cotton, the chairs were cushioned, and comfortable enough for a four-hour dinner. The waiters, older gentlemen dressed in black with white shirts and bow ties, their order books tucked neatly in their belts at their back, stood at the ready. The water, served in stem glasses with little paper sleeves around the base so as not to drip water on one's shirt or dress while drinking, was room temperature, no ice.

Crystal glasses all around, Severus plateware, silver service knives, forks, and spoons.

The crusty Papa Saco bread was flown in daily from Letie's Culinaria in Lisbon. The Jamón Ibérico de Bellota, acorn fed. Pata negra was pared with a small minute glass of bone-dry Riesling.

The Jamón had been dry cured for four years from the Bodega, and recognized as some of the finest in the world. A burst of umami in a slice of hand carved Jamón Ibérico was an awakening for my whole desirous mouth. I lived for this kind of food, being raised where it was meat and potatoes. This was too good to be the "something missing."

Surely it wasn't the Osso Bucco, the veal shanks came from the succulent fields of salty Salicornia surrounding the verdant estuarial marshes of Bilbao. The Viareggio white wine, now mostly found in the Canary Islands, was aromatic, with orchard ripe flavors of pear, apple, and citrus, with a short musical unfolding Aria of a taste of spicy fennel. This pairing was exquisite with the assorted flower and field greens salad.

The Portuguese red, Touriga Franca, one of the top 100 red wines in the world, filled my mouth with visions of burros walking between rows of grapes under sapphire skies with rainbows.

Penedes Cava with a silky Crema Catalana did it for me. The supple softness of the Crema was soft as my own inner lip.

A sensual light mint aperitif, served with amuse-bouche of pine, walnut and filbert nuts, various raw pasteurized goat and cow cheeses served on beds of ash and straw, with comb honey and small crusts of toast.

What was that my friend said? Oh yes,

"The meal was lacking." This was incredible, not possible.

"What was lacking?" I asked him, wiping the small crumbs from my white shirt.

I told him, while the elegant old waiter with his polished little silver scoop cleaned our white table cloth, that I had enjoyed this sumptuous repast to my fullest desires.

He looked at me, cocking his head to one side and said,

"Women."

He told me this over supple Cohiba cigars and smallish demitasse sized cups of Turkish coffee, i.e., half grounds and honey sweet.

He said that he knew an aristocratic old school Spanish Count that had two lovely and nubile young daughters. Twins, he

said. That the old Count was seeking to educate them "in the sweet ways of the Mus-
es." The old Count was married late in life,
to a young Basque-Spanish woman. A real
black-haired beauty, also from Spanish roy-
alty. The Count told my dear dinner com-
panion that he and his wife had settled on
him as the perfect mentor to wine, dine, and
sexually educate his daughters.

They were to sleep with us on the old
castle estate, all on the up and up, so said
my friend. The twins were 16 years old,
holding the quivering flushed promise of
youthful passion. This wasn't so unusual in
haute Spanish culture.

I listened, growing more and more uncomfortable. I replied at the end of his solil-
oquy by saying no.

"Why?" he asked, hardly believing I
had said no, his eyes wide.

"Simple," I said. "I am not in love with
either of them, including the mother. It isn't

sex for me, it must be love."

He looked at me and shook his head in severe disbelieve, while taking a long draw on his cigar.

"In that case, I will see you in the morning. Two for one," he winked.

If you are sweetie this, sweetie that all the time, stop reading now. This isn't for you unless you are just curious. Nothing wrong with being curious, just this may not be for you.

Bitter, of course I am bitter, I am a mortal human just like you, aren't I? Aren't you?

Judith adored eating. Something I understood. Give me a woman with appetite. Oh God, I was so instantly naive when I met her. Young love, what madness. Young or old we are all like spring calves when we are first smitten, ditzy.

"Taste," her first word when I met her in her jasmine covered beach cottage out on Arch Cape, Oregon. Arch Cape thrusts out to the continually rolling Pacific Ocean, near Cannon Beach, Oregon.

Her cottage was the color of the famous French piano, the powder blue Pleyel. The paint was scoured by wind borne sands, the white window trim had sandblasted streaks of grey.

Her first act upon meeting me was to shove a piece of scalding hot king salmon into my mouth. It tasted of Luxardo maraschino cherry and alder smoke. It was oily, while simply being seasoned with sweet Luxardo cherry juice, butter, salt, and pepper.

She was cooking this delectable king with black bean sauce and English cucumbers. The majestic king was served rare.

I remember that first meeting, for it unceasingly changed my life, minute by minute, hour by hour, day by day, years stood on end and today.

"Memories are hunting horns whose

noise dies away in the wind."

We own our memories and remembrances. I remember one thing clearly from that now long-ago day: her scent. Her scent that day was of expensive perfume, maybe overlaid with the primal smell of alder smoke, Luxardo cherry, and one more not so subtle, the pungent primal unpolished smell of her florid blossoming sex.

She was most always nude beneath her dresses. She always smelled like the intensely old-fashioned sweet viburnum. Old-fashioned fragrances, redolent of grown women.

She served each of us little overflowing glasses of Norwegian Linnea Schnapps. The Schnapps taken across the equator and back to improve its flavor in casks on the decks of ships. Not sweet schnapps, but rather the aquavit of Scandinavians, a lot more like vodka.

Her parties each started with a special

shot glass filled to the very rim and then some, a "bubble top."

"Pick your glass," she said as she swung open her cupboard filled to the edge with a sparkling glistening reef of fascinating glasses.

Most were hand made. Some were etched, some hammered in silver and gold. She was a collector of many things, glasses chief among them. There were little glasses she said she had bought on the Trans-Siberian Railway. These glasses, she said, were handed up to her open train window from peasants standing in the snow and dark, out in the wilds of Mother Russia. There were handmade Venetians rolled in 24 carat gold leaf, clay ones from Mexico, delicate blown flutes in silver holders from Paris, a grand and impressive assortment.

"Choice makes a difference. Make your choice," she said. Her tone wasn't always friendly, and in fact it was more often than not acerbic.

We gunned straight shots of ether laden aquavit in these rare shot glasses, elbow held high, Russian style, followed with Tuborg beer chasers, followed by dill-flavored chunks of homemade gravlax and more Schnapps.

When you start a party by knocking back three or four shots of aquavit and a couple of beers everything takes on a surreal appearance.

Aquavit seems to put an icy rime on the edge of a room, the windows, the candles, and everyone seems just a little bit closer in a distant way. A crystalline effect leans in on your temples while little pulses of rainbow light flutter, prancing in your peripheral vision.

Somehow the world clears up in an edgy way.

After our "petite snaps," as Judith called them, she served grilled blackened red Toltec peppers filled with chèvre, honey braised lamb shanks, Spanish saffron style rice, fresh garden cucumber, and watercress salad. Well, enough, I am sure you get the idea.

Her culinary arts snagged my eye. She was passionate about food as well as life, but that didn't make her any less difficult. If anything, more difficult. You probably know the bon mot, "Eccentrics are nice to know, hell to live with."

Her low-cut blouse, revealing her full breasts, sometimes a nipple, all caught my eye that first day. Her style of dress was casual while revealing her often naked body beneath thin dresses.

Her wine cellar was filled with wines from around the globe, the great vintages collected by her father and his father. She had a selection that included wines from the decades of the century, 1929 Bordeaux's, wines from the 1980s, whites of immense dignity, playful little Pinots, sauternes rich, filled with sun and sweet dreams. She also collected wines, as did her father, from around the world.

Her favorites being the wines of the Priorat in Catalunya in northeastern Spain, then France and California, and the unusual Pinotage of South Africa's west cape.

One of her favorite Priorats was called Scala Dei, Stairway to Heaven.

We sat talking, smoking Cubans, drinking a rare 1945 Porto so old that the color had changed from deep tawny red to clear. As we sat she told the story of how Scala Dei got its name.

"One day," she began, "there was a young peasant boy who dressed in a ragged straw hat, a coarse light blue muslin shirt, dark blue pants, and, barefoot, was going across the Mont Sant, west of Tarragona, Spain, to his village with exciting news.

"He had stopped at his favorite resting

place as usual during his weekly journey, because each time he stopped for his siesta, he dreamed of the Scala Dei.

"This then," she told us, "is the story he told while sitting on an old two wheeled wagon in the dusty farmyard surrounded by his mother, father, sisters, and brothers, as well as chickens, ducks, and goats who were all leaning in to hear his story.

"Walking along, thinking of God's blessings, leading his small limping goat, he said he spied on a hill above a small valley filled with ancient ruins his friend, the great tall tree reaching its limbs and top far into the azúl Spanish sky that he knew so well.

"Walking to the base of the noble grandfather giant, he led his small limping goat to a quiet place to rest its sore hoof, a place with water and grass. He was a good and thoughtful boy.

"Staking out his goat with a long-worn

rope, he walked to the base of the mighty soft moss and grass carpeted tree and lay down in the heat of the day in the shade of his friend, the great grandfather tree. Taking off his wide brim straw hat, the little lad laid his small head and back against the massive sloping side of the tree.

"Its leafy canopy caused shadows to flutter and dance on him. Putting his straw hat over his face, he closed his eyes. He could hear the sweet soft sounds of mewing lambs. Inside his hat he could smell the soap he had washed his hair with that morning. He could smell the straw from the hat and his own sweat. He was very comfortable and contented.

"He slept the sleep provided only to the very young and the very old.

"Sleep had taken him when in his vivid dreams he saw his mother, he saw his goat, little spotted Perla, and the wooden ladder that he had made that lead into the sky atop the barn to his dove cot.

"In his dreams he saw his dogs, Carlos, Rico, and Roja, running to him, licking his hands and face.

"He awoke, taking off his straw hat, and saw that it was his little limping goat that had grazed over to him and was licking his salty face. He put his hat back over his face and felt his little goat curl and lie down beside him, softly sighing. He could hear her gently chewing her cud.

"He breathed in that deep breath that infants do just before they let go, falling into deep sleep.

"Back in his dream world he instantaneously felt like the earth was falling out from under him, and he was powerless to stop tumbling in space. Falling through endless sky, he saw Perla, knees first, then hind legs and back, lay down in the soft green grass by his side while it champed its cud with the sweet grass, all in his dreams, a replay.

"The boy dreamed on and kept plunging down in terror. He called his mother.

"It was then he heard his mother's voice, heard her say out loud, very near his ear,

"'Oro,' then she was saying something else.

"He tried to get nearer to hear her, but she kept receding. He called to her, and she looked at him with great warmth, smiling and saying,

"'Oro.'

"Putting out his arms, he found that he could fly and settle down, landing near his mother. Walking now, he followed her until she stopped at the base of a very tall golden ladder. She stood behind the tall ladder with her right foot up on the first golden rung. Her face was framed by gold rungs. She beckoned again to him to follow her. He did, and they began to ascend the ladder. Mother, followed by her youngest son, up the golden ladder into the warm intense azúl Spanish sky.

"Picture this," Judith said.

"He could see his goat Perla receding at the bottom of the ladder as he climbed higher into the azúl sky. He could see his mother up ahead of him, sometimes so far that he lost sight of her in the clouds. She always waited for him to catch up. She was so kind.

"He saw their village priest walking with small children, all holding hands, some of whom he knew, in the clouds.

"He saw Christ's cross on a distant mote in the sky, heard the guitars of village dances. He saw smiling faces.

"Soon the Spanish earth disappeared. Mother and son climbed further into the sky. The ladder soon had no top, no bottom.

"Finally, after climbing through days and nights, his mother stopped. Climbing faster, he caught up with her. She was standing on the top rung where she thrust her arms out in a grand gesture, murmuring softly, sweetly, 'Look, look! We found the Scala Dei, Escalera al oro de los dioses en el Cielo. Stairway to God's Golden Heaven.'"

We were quiet for a while after this tale as Judith opened a vintage bottle of Scala Dei Cartoxia.

"Today," Judith said, "on the spot where the little shepherd boy had his dream, there now stands a white Spanish marble monastery, nearby the oldest wine cellar in northeastern Spain, which was begun by monks in the 12th century A.D. after hearing this legend."

Tipping gentle pours all around, smoking a short dark cigar clenched in her perfect white teeth, Judith poured everyone else's wine, then mine, looked at me, then winked.

Complicated. Did I say that? If I didn't,

I'm saying it now. She was complicated.

Her wood stove, a monstrous old Round Oak Chief, was laden with sauces-potpourris, some cooking for days and nights.

She chopped her own wood and kindling. Around this stove was a heat wave. It was always hot. Behind the stove, up against the warm wall on the warmer fir floor, her dog, Aston Martin, a coffee brown Irish Terrier, slept on his back in heedless slumber.

Her kitchen was the heart and sensual center of the chamber she called "the opening."

"Everything starts with food, it's all oral. When in doubt, feed them." These were her guides.

"It is all so elementary," she stated. "Try to remember your first nipple as an infant at your mother's breast. Food. You cried, you ate, so simple, yet so complicated. Unbelievably so. We never forget our earliest infant hunger, or the suckling filling of nurturing breast milk, and if we are highly fortunate, love, but then luck's a chance."

Judith's stove, a grand black chrome polished locomotive, sitting red hot, trivets piled with sauces, the reservoir steaming away, the firebox snapping out a tempo for cornbread in 12 short acts.

"Cook cornbread at 500 degrees for 10 minutes. Put fresh corn kernels and crushed filberts in the batter. It comes out tasting nutty."

Looking out an ornate patterned leaded window through the stoves shimmering heat was her well-tended garden, filled with garlic, garlic chives, lemon thymes, Korean mint, oregano, raspberry bushes, strawberries, blueberries, carrots, beets, salad greens, and a wide variety of rare herbs and vegetables.

She controlled her kitchen, which faced west over the white capped jadeite Pacific, the same way an artist controls a pallet or a conductor his orchestra.

She flourished forks and spatulas as though they were brushes and batons. Broad impassioned emblazoned saucy strokes across the plates of her kitchen, splatters and drips, bits and pieces were eaten by all of us hovering like gulls around a herring ball.

"Taste this," another spatula shoving scalding potato au gratin at my mincing mouth. To be cute this time she wiped the oily spatula across my nose and winked.

"I like you," she said. My heart jumped.

"Here," she said, giving me a very sharp butchers knife. "Dice this, peel those tomatoes, make tomato con casa for me! Little triangles, make sure the seeds are out! What, you have never made tomato con casa?"

She had a way of looking when she couldn't believe that the rest of the world didn't know everything she knew, even though she was ever arrogant about what she knew and you didn't.

"Troll caught."

What?

"The king salmon was troll caught this morning off the Astoria bar."

"I grow the Thai peppers and English cukes. Easy to grow, only trick is consistency with watering."

She was full of tidbits of knowledge.

"Never turn fish on the grill," she once told me. "When the fish starts to bubble little white bubbles on top, take it off immediately, and it will finish cooking on the way to the table."

"Blacken peppers slowly. Put them in a warm garlic rubbed dish, cover with parchment paper for an hour, and the skin slips off by itself."

"Use your hands when you cook. Feel the food, eat with your hands, suck your fingers. Here," she said once, mixing chocolate with her hands, "suck mine."

"Mix the salad with your fingers. Use the mad woman method. Roll the gnocchi with rhythmic forward and backward movements. Grab the capon by the raw neck, reach inside its anus, and pull out its guts."

"To as great a degree as sexuality, food is inseparable from imagination."

"Imagination is the conveyer of clarity in all elevated creative thought."

"Think food, think sex. Every cause, every action is transferable. You can build meaning on that."

"Start with the big muscles when you massage. Use warm scented oils. Feel the need. Be the person you are massaging. Rub slowly, stretch me out. Women aren't men. Roll me over, elongate, take away my contracted thoughts, slowly. Men are always in such a hurry. Think of my soft white belly as a joint of beef. Fall in love with it and sweetly massage round and round and more. Use your nose or your ear or your tongue, make me unique. If you want to make love to me in the evening, start in the morning."

All of this and more she later told me as we stood in the surf looking back at the candle lit house, standing among the head high sea grasses. I looked over at her, dazzled by her beauty, as an incoming wave pulled at her sheer silk skirt, swirling, revealing her wet dark delta indented at her thighs.

I reached across the foaming Pacific, embracing her cold, goosebump covered body, closed my eyes, kissing her hard as that towering, rolling, phosphorescent wave lifted us off the bottom, washing us ashore amid the rolling surf. We held each other like mating jellyfish, tumbling in the dark sandy scouring bed of the endless Pacific. We washed up, and as the wave subsided on that drift filled beach, her heated salty tongue, licking my eyes, my cheeks, finally found its way to my thrilled mouth. God, what strength flowed through me. Can I? Yes, I can and do feel like one of those great Columbia silver king salmon, all muscle.

If you were going to be around Judith, she showed as well as told you a lot, but that wasn't bad, really, because she knew a lot. Her fascination was with life, her curiosity was never still.

She couldn't be less than she was!

Judith's beach cottage, surrounded by blue green dune grasses, was a dimensional Persian rug filled with an eclectic array of art. The interior of the cottage was older dark fir, smoked for ages by the great and gigantic fireplace at the end of her living room. Kitchen, bathrooms, laundry, attic, behind the couch, the walls, floors, under the bed, everywhere seemed to be some rare painting, sculpture, ceramic, or some varied thing of interest.

In the kitchen attached to the wall were

finely wrought varnished wooden cubicles, embellished in which were ancient Indian baskets, a rare Tibetan Chang jug, Benin Bronzes, skulls, Indian trade beads, small dishes of carved Eskimo ivories, antique statuary, and hot blown glass, an eclectic and thought-provoking colorful assortment. Paintings jammed the walls, French salon style, closets, behind the sofas.

Hers wasn't a house where all of the magazines were lined up parallel to the corners of the coffee table, where all was neat and aligned. It was controlled, fascinating chaos with museum quality objects everywhere.

Through her windows the wind and rain runnel her sculpture garden. Her flower and vegetable gardens were all silhouetted against the western Pacific Ocean. Vast rich carved basalt columns, hard-edged patinated bronzes, pools with fountains reflecting and refracting the saline sky all encrusted her home.

She was one of those rare people who thought life can always be better if consumed fresh.

Enough was never enough for this Judith, for whom enough was too little.

She was an artist who lived an artistic experience. There were few boundaries in her, and that was her sculpture and her strength. She was her art. No one else really mattered to her. She controlled most everyone around her with the force of her will power.

Her whole life was art, fine on the surface, but hard to live with. Step into her life and she was instantly two up on you. She gave nothing back, not even a borrowed book.

With her there was no place to hide. Pardon the banality of this, but with her it was her way or the highway.

I suppose she still means something to

me, but there I go again. You see, forgetting is hard for me with her. When I think of her now, however, I feel like a half-finished artwork. She chipped, chiseled, gessoed, stretched, sanded, patinated, welded, hammered, and still left me unfinished.

However, who's to say what's finished? I lived and died so many times in her arms. I think she tried to use me up.

I think to be finished with her was out of the question. Nothing was finished in her life. There was no beginning, no ending, just a smear, shards of colored light and dense twisting dark vertigo.

She had sexual passion as you might guess from what I've told you. Wild, unbridled, the kind I could rock my bones to.

"I'm your little Blackfoot maid," she would say.

She liked to bite me, little nips all day just to make me think about that hot little tent in her great soft bed. Her feather quilt dazzled and broken like sunlight over her back.

Her nakedness was naked.

Did you ever notice some people look like they were born to walk around naked? Then some are quivering, mincing, uncomfortable with their nude naked bareness. When walking in light, shining, illuminating light, they hold their hands over their sex, hoping, seeking darkness, any way to avoid being seen. Some people retire into a fragrant twilight hiding.

Then others advance, as did the Vikings, into love and war. No armor, no cloths, only a sword or spear and an erection, this was Judith, clitoral.

To endeavor to forget Judith was a certain way of thinking of nothing and no one else but Judith.

Oh Judith, tell me, do you love me? Tell me, so I can live or die. With love comes insanity.

"Runner" was the vanity license plate on Judith's car. This car, among several that she owned, was one of her prize possessions. It was a Stirling Moss green 1952 MG-TD, rickety and brittle as an old maid aunt and as crotchety and breakable as a porcelain teacup. Runner had 16-inch wire wheels that shuttered and shook if you drove over 70 miles per hour.

We were on a road trip one time in Runner going up into the Yellow Stone Park country. In her attempt to sound Scandinavian and cute, she called it "Jelly Stone." God, I hated that! Don't ask me why that got to me, but it's like someone asking you which way you wipe. So what?

She could be so pitifully boring with that kind of drivel, then in the next moment she would say something like,

"Did you know that Nijinsky, the Russian Ballet, and Charlie Chaplin all danced together in Hollywood, then at St. Petersburg's Mariinsky Theatre?" Ah no, I didn't know that.

Her car was unsafe, I told her that more than once. She denied it, which was usually the case with her. She denied everything, then thought about it, or not!

"Consistency is the hobgoblin of small minds," she said. She always had little sayings for what seemed to me for every facet of life.

Well, anyway, I got use to most of it. Finally got to enjoy her thoughts. I enjoyed her ways. I loved her ways. God, I wanted to hate her ways, but, well, that was a part of the territory.

When I went to her beach house, she liked to meet me at the door, sensing my arrival someway, somehow, way before I would even so much as knock.

I see her now with the warm woodsy slightly smoky air flowing around her silk dress with rich candlelight, transparent, outlining her nude shape beneath. Being the artist and rebel she was, she rarely wore anything under her silk dresses.

She loved candles and candelabras, lanterns and fireplaces. Because of this her home was alive in shadows at night.

She stood there at her hand carved door, just slightly on my side of the door jam. Her hand on my chest, holding me away, and looked me over, top to bottom for a stilled, silent moment, suppressing, it seemed, a great burst of merriment before letting me in.

"Hello there," she would say in her rich way, then smile while covering her mouth with a long pale elegant hand. Her nails were natural as was she, no lipstick or rouge. She contained great strata of natural coloring. She would then break out laughing. Rich, ripe, tonal sounds with that mouth, teeth, tongue. How beautiful and seductive.

In the next moment clutch me hard,

looking up imploringly, whimpering.

The portal, the door, the gate, the abstract opening, all were so important to her. She greeted men like a feral vixen, curling, smiling, insinuating, nipping. A greeting few understood, but almost all recognized. Her ways were ripe, full peaches, summer penduline. She was blooming every half-hour, and it wasn't a secret.

Thinking of her and that car makes me think again of our Yellow Stone trip.

We had left the Pacific Northwest, drenched in 100 different kinds of rain. On the fenders our canvas duffels were covered in large plastic garbage sacks to protect our belongs against the rain. Inside the small humid car, we attempted with duct tape, rags, and cardboard to keep out the driving rainwater that flowed through every small crack. The top, the body, the doors, the fold down windshield, they all dribbled and gushed from every crack, and there were many.

Judith's car was an antique. 1952 was a long time ago. This old machine was delicate. Its walnut dash was studded with gauges, knobs, toggle switches, and in the dark it all glowed red like some old tube radio. The insufficient microscopic heater broiled our feet just at the heater, while our upper bodies froze. The windshield wipers were mounted to the outside top of the windshield. They went faster when the engine was speeding downhill and came to a full stop when we were laboring up the many mountain passes as we traveled east towards Twin Falls, Idaho on highway 20, then over Targhee Pass heading for Yellow Stone Park. While heading east over the Cascade mountains, we were awash in water as trucks sped past, leaving us spectacularly soaked. We drove with plastic tarps in our laps to repel the rain leaking from every small hole in the top. As we drove south and east through the Rockies, the weather began to change from dry to warm to hot. As we began to dry out, we stowed the canvas top in the trunk, letting the warm spring breezes fill and eventually dry out the inside of the damp car, pulling the coastal damp from our cloths, as well as putting sunlight on our welcoming faces. Costal firs and cedars were replaced with quaking aspen, dancing hot dust devils in plowed fields, red willow, beaver ponds, and lava fields with ancient cypress.

The smell of hot asphalt, engine oil mixed with dust, and sage all smelled of the high prairie. Where before all was dark and rain-fog and mist in the west, now was sunny with fields of grain and cattle. Hawks hunted the fields while meadowlarks sang from old rusty barbwire fences.

Feedlots and small towns dotted the plains. White farmhouses with windmills. Barns out back with corrals and horses and cattle in distant pastures. Behind old barns and outbuildings were junked cars, out of date combines, tractors, hay bailers, and more. It seemed the farmers/ranchers never threw anything away.

As we traveled on into the mountains we came to the entrance to Yellow Stone Park. Driving for some time deeper into the park, we rounded one long sloping curve amid dense small black pines heading up into Old Faithful Country and the famous Yellow Stone Lodge.

Rounding the curve, we came to an abrupt stop behind a short line of cars. Sitting in Runner, which had the top stowed in the trunk and from which I could easily reach out and touch the ground, I watched with a feeling of terror ripping my flesh as five big black bears, drunk on junk food, marched single file around the car in front of us, trailing a runty little cub. The windows on that car were rolled up to a slit through which the children inside were variously pushing out food of all sorts and jabbing at the bears with a stick. The bears in turn were pawing at the car and licking the windows. Trying to get at the food, they wheezed like old, out of shape wrestlers gnawing on each other. The mother and father, that would be the children's guardian parents of this motley bunch, were laughing uproariously while the driver, the dad, honked the car horn often to make the bears jump. Sometimes he roared and revved up his engine to frighten the bears while engulfing us in a grey blizzard of exhaust.

The unhealthy-looking runty cub spying Judith and me in our open car sauntered back toward us with several of the other bears following. This all took place in seconds. Bears look pretty big when you are sitting at their feet out in the open. Judith, who was talking and looking at me, saw the change in my plate-sized eyes. She turned, looked, saw the bears, said

"Jesus Christ," and gunned Runner around in the middle of the road, just missing one of the bears that was placidly eating pretzels.

I think she hit the bear standing next to the first; however, it was hard to determine whether she actually hit it or if he had just taken a playful swing at us as we nearly drove over its claws.

That was a quality I liked about her. She could perform in an emergency.

Another quality I detested was her ability to be unbelievably ugly at any time, for no reason. Waitresses were live bait.

I pulled off the two-lane road into a gravel parking lot of a smallish old farm-style restaurant-bar held up by piers over the Yellow Stone. Judith was impossible all day, gloomy. It was late in the day and we both were famished. Sitting down at a small table by a window with a flashing neon sign attached, we looked at the greasy menu. I was about to order a beer when Judith shouted across the room.

"Any specials on the menu? It's so greasy I can't read the damn thing!"

"It's all in the menu," said the tired old waitress.

"I didn't ask you that, now did I?" shouted Judith, curling her lip. "What's on the fucking menu? Any specials?"

"It's all in there, today's specials too," said the waitress.

"What does it say? Who can read this through the grimy fingerprints?" Judith asked.

"Look, it's all there," said the waitress.

"God damn your ears, tell us what the specials are or we are gone!"

"There's the door!" shouted the old tired waitress. "Please let it hit you in your broad fat ass."

I wanted to laugh, it was really funny,

but then that day wasn't funny in any way.

With that little bit of nonsense on very empty stomachs, in the middle of the night, in the middle of a great dark wilderness, Judith swept the table. The napkin holder, ketchup bottle, mustard, toothpicks, lotto cards, menus, bread plate, everything shattered on the floor. While stalking toward the door, Judith yelled at the old waitress,

"What a fucking hag!"

The cook, a burly young logger type, came out of the kitchen at the noise. The old waitress shouted back the moment Judith passed angrily through door,

"Put it where the sun doesn't shine, Sweetie."

Judith stormed out, swearing into the dark beautiful mountainous valley. The cook followed us out to the porch and said he was calling the sheriff if we didn't get the hell out of there, pronto.

"You God damn slickers." Judith

turned, giving him the finger. I grabbed her arm, pulling her to our car.

The car, still hot and popping, was sitting under the dark star tracked dome of sky. It was all so lovely. I could hear coyotes singing songs of love in the verdant pine forest in the hills behind the bar. Somewhere, an owl.

Elegant dinner parties were more than once turned into free-for-alls because of her. She was never sorry, you took her the way you got her. For the most part it was great, but my God when it wasn't.

It's hard to describe this crazy woman, or at the least hard for me. Forest for the trees. You may know someone like this.

Certain invective, certain sophisticated types of behavior coupled with a sort of obscene grossness that was attracting and repelling, sometimes at the same time, sometimes singularly. The sting, the determined bear, and that glorious sweet, sweet honey.

She was a little older than me. Her hair was on the brittle side unless she was at the ocean, where it quieted down to a rich luxuriant brown pelt. Her eyes were unsettling. Blank at times like a gecko, though like the gecko she adored in a compelling way, laughing in the predawn darkness. The roar of constant surf and the slamming vibration of the pounding surf outside her beach house jared against her sex in a jellied, sensual way, a certain gravitational pull, something geologic.

When away from the sea she became edgy.

Nearly always in secure defense of herself, though always in some way desirous. A naked person moving in unpredictable physical and mental jerks through life.

Her large lips were nearly toothless feeling when kissing me, but when she was fully aroused her kisses covered my face in Watusi-like slaps.

Somehow, a certain laughter entered into her squirming lovemaking. She had a way of wrapping me in shadow fingered embracing acts of love that unsettled me to the core. I gurgled and gasped under eyes that never lost their lack of love.

Salt cavern storm surges rolled up her thighs and broke in laughter across her coral parted lips.

Her sometimes loud moans, screaming cries, broke through my deafened joy like distant birdcalls across hot jungle canyons.

Her parents, now dead, had been great successes in the world. They were educated, moneyed, moved in the most important circles of power in the swamp lands of Washington, D.C. Her father, a congressional attorney, wrote the first legislation making the moon neutral territory for the nations of the world. His litigate stories were legend. Her mother, from a wealthy Louisiana lumber family, was thin, shrill, of French-

Irish ancestry. She forced herself through a life that seemed to offer little in the way of lightness. Both were heavy smokers, Camels and Lucky Strikes, and even heavier drinkers. Gin with Listerine chasers before lunch and gin gunned down with beer chasers after lunch. They lurched through their successful professional daily lives barely surviving each day's charade. Tumbling from their chauffeured black limousine onto the stoop of their aristocratic Washington, D.C. apartment building, they careened into elevators, stumbled down elegantly appointed hallways to their palace-like apartment. Once seated there in splendid disarray, each in their own large chair, each with their own large gin, each with their own cigar and cigarette, they shouted, harangued, and cursed each other until they passed out. Cigar and cigarette burns littered the priceless oriental carpets around them.

Occasionally her mother, drunk and

outraged at the whimpering of her small daughter in her distant bedroom suite, would pass by the royal rosewood sideboard, grab a handful of elephant ivory handled steak knives, and make an unsteady run at the 12-foot-high French doors to the nursery.

She would rip open the doors, stand there in the glare, an ugly bat for a shadow, and throw knives at the dim, distant crib, drunkenly shouting, "Shut up, shut up, shut up!"

Chapter 2

One night up on the Yellow Stone River as we lay close in bed in a little log cabin motel, our day passed through my mind. The tears on her cheeks were now dried to little salt crystals. I held her with my leg over hers while cradling her body wrapped in my arms. Sounds of the river, fragrant and near, the soft repeated calls of an owl somewhere, staring into the dark as I was, mice rummaging in the rafters, all lulled my turbulent thoughts. Thinking of the day I flushed, then angered once more for a moment, then the night worked its magic and I let it go.

She had been hell all day. Now she slept after crying for an hour in front of the large old soot-stained river rock fireplace holding my knees.

Her bare breasts were against my legs as she sat on the dark pine floor, an old Hudson Bay blanket wrapped partly around her. Looking up at me, she made me promise I wouldn't leave her and go home.

She made me promise I wouldn't make her sleep alone, something that terrified her. When alone she slept with the lights on, while a radio played soft classical. I looked down at her, cradling her until she slept. Her face when she was sleeping like this, after intense torment, was angelic, a Botticelli innocent, her flush pink cherub cheeks, a walnut brown lock of hair over her right eye.

From early that fresh splendid morning, traveling in Runner, top down at 70 miles per hour through some of the most beautiful sage and pine mountains I had ever the pleasure to see, country that should have inspired while drawing us close, she grew more and more petulant, while insanely petty. Instead of stopping to make love on our handmade Montana quilt under quaking aspens down by fragrant rivers in flowered meadow bottoms, we raced, fast, she pushing us along, her mood petulant and surly. I tried words of love, levity, sensual touches to the back of her now arched neck, anything to turn back the maelstrom of dark water. The rising black tide of hate rising from her lips clouded her eyes, filled her vision. She looked, seeing pitchy gloom.

Fields filled with lowing golden-colored cows, foxes jumping after small mice, elk bugling, all fresh and filled with life contrasted with the ugly cloud inside the desperate little car.

I said, "I love you."

She said, "Die."

I said, "I love the smell of the hills."

She said, "Stick it."

I tried, "I love our travels together."

She said, "Piss on it all."

I pleaded, "Please can we stop this?"

She spit at me, but the wind carried her spit up and off onto the fragrant valley air.

She started again with the car thing, knowing she was saying nothing but beating me with her extreme agitation, telling me how wonderful, how safe her car was as we ripped along, our lives at risk, near jagged dark basalt cliffs fronting sharp edged river drop-offs.

It wasn't what she said but as always with her her tone, how she said it. Judith had the ability to be breezy, airy, sarcastic with acerbic vitriol and smiling, knowing while laughing she was spreading gloom. I was driving way too fast. With her I always drove too fast because she only wanted to drive fast. She liked everything at its peak risk point, the hell with longevity, as she put it. 25 miles per hour through small rural towns was misery for her.

"How do you spell accelerate?" she shouted in my ear so loudly it made it ring.

On this day where the sky invited you to touch its beauty, a day as exquisite as young love, a day where each breath of mountain air was sensual and life giving, we careened out of a 90 degree twisted road cut, the tires squealing and complaining. The road straightened, disappearing over the distant mountain-filled horizon, the snow-scented Yellow Stone racing us side by side.

"Step on it, asshole. Are you at least able to do that? Hey shit hook, I'm talking to you!" she screamed.

Her incredible agitation snapped, broke, crushed my mental resolve to cherish this day and not to let it vanish from my grasp, but it was over after days of hell, and tiny, very little minute bits of heaven. My nerves felt like a handful of telephone wires ripped from a wall. Her black ink dark mood stirring the cauldron inside my heated skull finally worked its sick magic.

I let go of my resolve to survive this life in one piece, and jammed, crammed with all of my might at the delicate little antique gas pedal. The engine leaped in a way that surprised me. The river, broken rocks, fence posts, clouds of insects, small birds, telephone poles, everything outside of the car started to blur like approaching death.

The speedometer pegged. She, thank God, stopped talking. She clutched her leather door handle for some kind of safety, her hair blowing wildly, uncontrolled around her fearful face, madly staring down the road in terror.

She was tough, but my mood had now

also turned ugly, even more than I could control. In a word I lost it. I resolved not to say a word, even as the car started to go out of control, she finally couldn't swallow her terror.

"Slow down!" she anxiously shouted into the roar of the wind. I didn't.

"You son of a bitch," the words bull-whipped out of her mouth as she eyed my foot mashed on the gas pedal. "You pathetic bastard," ricocheted off the vibrating wooden dash, disappearing into the speeding wake of our slipstream, like bullets overhead.

"Listen dummy, dip dong, puke faced stump brain, stop! This is my car." Her face was shaking and inches from mine but she didn't dare touch me as she could easily see it was harder and harder for me to keep control of the increasingly vibrating, oscillating, rickety sewing machine of a car. The front wheels, which were a little out of balance at 70 miles per hour, now rattled the whole front of the car at 90.

"When we get near an airport you are out of my life you motherless bastard!" she screeched. She was frightened with good reason, her wide eyes in helpless terror were trying to get attention out of my grim set face and white clenched jaw. She was having no success.

The left front wheel started to leap on and off the blacktop as a hub cap came off on its own, bouncing down into the pristine salmon spawning grounds of the river as we screamed past, starting to lose parts like a re-entry vehicle from space. Next the hood-latch snapped open on her side and started to flop wildly in the hurricane blowing by the car.

At that moment she snapped, tears driven back along her ears, certain death was coming her way. Coming somewhat back to my senses, I was coming to see that this could end in something worse than another bitter argument. I was getting nervous. I had flashes in my thoughts of our destroyed, dead, bleeding bodies in a cheap little morgue in Wyoming, where only old dead famers had laid before.

Time, in one of those funny little moments while furious action goes on all around, stopped. At this precise moment, she grabbed my favorite hat off my head throwing it onto the slipstream, howling over the windshield, while crying a bawling noise like a lacerated calf. Next she reached behind me, grabbed my leather jacket, and jettisoned it over the side at the blur of pavement. My white duffel bag tied onto the fender on her side was next. She jerked open the lanyard, reached in, and grabbed handfuls of my shorts, t-shirts, overnight bag, anything she could lay her hands on, and tossed them all off onto the wind. I was screaming by this time. I locked all four wheels in a blue rubber smoking uncontrolled sideways stop in the middle of the road. As we slid sideways, two wheels on one side came up off of the pavement, the whole car hung there a moment then banged back down. The engine was smoking and still running.

The world got very quiet for a moment, blue rubber smoke swirling around us. Somewhere a meadowlark sang. Then I ground the goddamned car into reverse so hard I wanted to break it. Jesus, I was mad. I backed up as fast as a MG-TD would whine in reverse, backing right over my overnight bag where it lay bleeding cologne. I looked up to see a car swerve to miss my leather jacket, which had the appearance of a roadkill. I jerked on the emergency brake, stood up in the red leather seat, spit at Judith, yelling,

"Bitch!" and jumped over the low door out of the car into the disheveled line of my belongings strewn for several blocks along the riverbank road. I reached down, picking up a t-shirt.

Of course, when I was out of the car I was so mad that I hadn't realized I had forgotten to take the key. As I started picking up my belongings, I turned as I heard Judith crank the engine, chortling and yelling,

"Good riddance, you son of bitch!" as she drove off, giving me the constant finger until she disappeared around a bend a mile further down the canyon.

It was quiet, I was alive, the clouds were white and lofty, the meadowlarks were singing as the river purled softly, and for the moment I needed a reality check. Who was I, where was I, and why was I? What had just happened? I wanted to rage, I wanted to cry, I was glad I was alive, I was glad Judith was gone. What's the saying, "Here are me."?

"Where are me?" I wondered.

The air was heavy with the dry smell of summer grass, the Yellow Stone, jade green washed over small mossy rocks, ducks floated along, somewhere a cow bawled out, a hawk screamed high overhead a dog barked, then another dog answered. I finally found my favorite hat at the head of my belongings that had been strewn along the little country road.

I headed back up the road in the direction we were headed. In the distance, snow-capped mountains glistened pink in the late afternoon sun.

I walked along, breathing in the fragrance of the hay fields, the river, the sense of peace. Clasping my cloths to my chest, shirt sleeves hanging down, sweaters and jeans around my neck, everything smelling like the cologne bottle that I had crushed as I backed up over it.

I walked for about an hour in the gathering darkness while the fragrant dry farm air had turned to damper evening air. I could hear the descending evening cry of the robin, ducks gabbling, dogs barking, cow bells, a whole melody of early twilight sounds.

I walked for that hour without seeing another car before an old '54 5 window Chev half-ton pickup truck swerved in my direction, stopping beside me at the side of the road. After the fresh agricultural smell of the land, the truck brought with it the smell of exhaust and hot engine oil.

I watched as the man inside the old truck reared back, kicking the door open on the passenger side, and asked if I needed a drink and a ride. I nodded, threw my armful of belongings into the middle of the seat next to a large but friendly looking pugnacious mutt and climbed in.

"Overland Pipes is the name and writing's my game. What the hell are you doing out here, Son? You look like a bag lady." He shoved a soft cotton candy pink hand the size of a catcher's mitt at me.

"How far have you been walking, Son? Where the hell did you come from? You smell of cologne, strongly, I might say," and he laughed, a gentle chuckling sound.

We drove off at about 10 miles per hour while he searched under the dog for something, swerving into the oncoming lane.

"Ha!" he yelped, pulling out a green two-liter bottle of sake. He pulled the cork and threw it out the window. "Now that you're here we won't be needing any cork," he said, and laughed in an infectious way. I looked at him and eyed the bottle.

"Ya I know, sake, but it was the last thing in the cupboard. You get used to it when you live as far into the hills as I do. Pretend that it's yeasty beer." And with that he shoved the bottle under the dog's nose to my side of the car. The dog licked the wet mouth of the jug as it was passed under his nose.

Drinking hot sake in Hinoki pine square wooden cups is one thing, location in a tatami mat room somewhere in Japan being everything. Swigging it out of a half-gallon sized tall green saki bottle in the hot oily interior of an old beat up farm truck up in Wyoming is totally another. I could see the pavement through the floorboards.

A line of cars that had built up behind us started to honk. Overland jerked the wheel to the right and stopped with me looking right down into the Yellow Stone, the whole truck defying gravity, my life hung out to dry on the thinnest, flimsiness of threads.

"Trouble is everybody's in a rush," he loudly said, with his arm out the window waving amicably for people to past. I took a long hit on the bottle then handed it back.

"Keeping baby warm," he said, caressing the bottle after a rather long cow-like slurp. He shoved the bottle back at me one more time, grinning all the while. I took another slug, passed it back by the dog that affectionately gave me a six-inch long tongue kiss on the lips. Somehow at that moment I didn't mind. My mood had calmed. Half an hour later the bottle took an air burial into the woods just before rounding a corner into a small-town clinging by its teeth between mountain and the Yellow Stone.

"Don't ever eat in this town," he said. "In fact, don't even stop in this town unless you want to drink, and in that case the Golden Horseshoe is for you." And then as an afterthought he said, "And me too," and poked the nose of the Chev in between two large muttering diesel log trucks whose bumpers were higher than the roof of his old Chev 5 window pickup truck.

The yellow neon sign on the front of the weathered building sizzled occasionally, flashing "-old-n -orsesho-".

"Stay in the truck, Pegasus," he ordered, but the dog jumped out and followed us up to the bar anyway. The outside of this rustic bar was built of dark bark covered logs. It had neon beer signs in the windows.

I found myself laughing for the first time that day as the sake, Overland and his dog Pegasus, and the bar all took on a hazy, slightly drunk, hilarious air. Out in the middle of the small dance floor an Indian man wrapped in fur with long gray braids danced with a tall husky dog in what looked like a quarter inch of gin.

The bar was covered in writhing bodies as thick as a breeding ground. I could only assume the bar was there. People were grabbing each other like monkeys picking fleas. Everything was bathed in purple light and smelled like a cross between a cheap restaurant, a rock concert, and just for the hell of it, throw in a shingle mill.

"Jesus, Overland what are you doing in here after breakfast?" a voice yelled above the jumble of noise.

As I looked for the owner of the voice, a hand shot up from the floor beside the crowded bar where a large man with horse-like purple teeth sat with a dark woman in the six-inch thick sawdust and peanut shells that covered the floor. The man was the color of the surrounding hills with a body as swelling as a draft horses ass. The woman looked like a purple stork folded up on her nest.

"Baker, hows the music business?" Overland shouted over Willie Nelson's "To All the Girls I've Loved Before".

"Florence, good to see you. How's your ma?" They both stood up, and my eyes must have shouted out what my mouth wouldn't, for Florence laughed loudly, lustily, and said something lost in the din to Baker who laughed as well.

Florence was taller by far than all of us, and Baker was a giant.

Her neck was covered in tattoos, from

the opening in her blouse to her chin, like a printed turtleneck. Her wrists and arms were covered with flower patterns, and her belly, which showed beneath her cutoff dark western shirt, was tattooed in an interlocking wreaths of red roses. She leaned over me, looked me straight in the eye, then pulled down her lower lip with a long polished black fingernail. Inside her soft pink lip her social security number was tattooed in green. We all laughed uproariously as she leaned close to my ear and shouted,

"And there's more."

"Howdy," Baker said to me. "You from around here?"

Before I could answer, Overland said,

"I picked him up on the river fork road gathering laundry."

Before I could explain that comment, Overland's dog tried to take the head off the dancing husky out on the dance floor. Baker leaped out on the floor and waded out into the middle of the fight, inadvertently knocking the dog's dancing partner to the floor. Grabbing a dog in each of his large hands, Baker propelled the husky in a smooth arc over the top of the bar into the bartender while Overland grabbed Pegasus by the scruff of the neck and the fur of his back half, dragging and carrying Pegasus, who was whining and scratching, out the front door toward the street. Over his shoulder he shouted back at Florence and Baker, saying,

"I just was going to buy this fellow a beer, but it's just too crazy for an old guy like me this time of night. Besides, it makes my hearing aids loudly ring."

Standing out on the porch while Pegasus relieved himself on a nearby truck tire, a drunk belched,

"Hey look, a dog suitcase."

Overland ignored them, clicking with his tongue while motioning to Pegasus to jump into the front seat.

"I thought that we might have time for a wee nip here, but this place gets too nuts for an old guy like me at this time of the day. The eagle flies, the booze flows, and while the big head gets drunk, the little head does the talking, if you catch my meaning."

He laughed warmly and turned, wrenching open the protesting driver's door.

An empty beer can rolled out onto the gravel of the parking lot as he put his foot on the running board. Turning, and in a warm deep voice said,

"Well Son, I think it's time I be getting' on upriver. Since you didn't find your friend, you are welcome to stay with me and Mavis at our place if you like."

"Thanks Overland, that is mighty kind of you, I'd like that," I said.

We climbed into the truck and headed out of the dirt parking lot and onto the little two-lane road heading out of town. A half mile or so down the moonlit Yellow Stone overhung by dark ponderosa pines, in a moon lit bend in the river I spotted the sign "Rustic Creek Cabins" and in front of the one nearest the river stood Runner with the driver's door open, the right red taillight blinking.

"Well, I will be damned, Overland, pull over here. I never thought I would ever see that woman again, but there she is, at least there's my ride. I sure want to thank you for the lift and your kind offer."

"It's okay, Son, just ask Frankie at the front desk where Overland lives, then in the morning pop on up for breakfast. Coffee is always on. Bonne chance, Son."

As I walked toward the cabin in the dark, I could see that all of the lights were on in the cabin. The big cedar plank door was closed. The hackles on the back of my neck sprang up and I jumped when a voice very nearby said,

"Don't ever do that to me again."

Judith was invisible, sitting in front of the closed dark door in an overstuffed chair she had pulled from inside the cabin. She was smoking a cigar, and as I got close, I could smell scotch on her breath, also the smell of a lot of crying. I thought of the many things I wanted to say to her: That her mental horsepower was out of control most of the time, like her car and I were earlier. That she lashed out in defense, crippling, destroying, and maiming, for whatever the cause, large or small, a cannon to kill a sparrow. That her lovemaking lacked love. That I was there because I was totally fascinated to the point of my own destruction but said none of them. I was in some sort of defense-less shock when I was with her, regardless of if it was a gun in my face or a breast in my mouth.

When I woke up in the morning she was

sitting up, watching me, waiting for me to wake up. She quietly pulled the quilt over her shoulders while she straddled me from a sitting position, pushed my softness into her, wrapping me in her body until I stiffened in her soft insides, intently watching me, she rocked her hips, gently putting me back to sleep.

A poor piece of architecture can make a beautiful ruin, and like my dear grandfather use to say,

"A woman's ass and a whiskey glass have made a horse's ass out of me."

Our lives were turbulent. She was turbulent. Judith was a boiling raging caldron of pain and pleasure.

Why was I always waiting?

It's a big world, there are other women, other places, but in those days it was only her. I wanted some days to run. I would tell myself that she didn't need me, and I don't think she did. Did I need her? A man shouldn't have to wait forever, and yet God damn it. God damn it.

Women.

How I love them, are they worth it? Shit, don't even listen to me, I'm not rational on this subject. Shall I be trite? Love is blind. Worse, love has no eyes whatsoever. But when she smiled or put her hand on the back of my neck, I loved it. To feel her pulling on my belt buckle or to have her put her hands on my hips. Yes, and yes.

Her intensity was the kind that just when I thought that I could respond with love-passion-intensity of my own she would disappear, somewhere just out of my reach, a Mona Lisa smiling all the time, holding her hand behind her back.

If whiskey was rainwater what a wonderful world it would be. How much to drink to still the pain, now there's a question. I could never drink enough to still the pain before I passed out.

The first time we slept together was after a wonderful meal at her Arch Cape house. This was the second time we had met, and she was, as usual, in her kitchen, working like a devil Goddess over her wood stove. She bent to pull open the oven door, and her blouse fell open, revealing her full, tantalizing breasts, silken, pendulous, flushed nipples, filled with her aromatic warmth.

A white-hot volt went through me. She pulled a pan of honey braised lamb shanks from the hot dark heat of the oven, noticed my eyes, and stood near me ostensibly to show me the lamb shanks when she knew, and I knew, she was showing her breasts. I leaned back, embarrassed at my instant desire. She leaned into me, looked into my eyes and understood, murmuring,

"Later."

Not that I was uncomfortable, she didn't notice, but understood my longing. I always longed for her, this she knew even then. She was sensual, appealing in ways, grace-filled with movement that wasn't learned, she was born that way.

I blunted my desire on her. To see her, react to her was my joy, however love, you know the blissful marital love, was not something she ever gave.

She could give me sex, animal, erotic, scratching, grasping, gasping, sexual madness when she wanted to. To sleep with her was one thing, but don't expect to talk about kids, church, marriage, or love, the Hallmark card type. She doled out her body sparingly, but at other times with great tidal surges when she came to me in her desire. My desire? Well not so much. Many nights she crested on the heaving, surging tidal waves of my desire while at other times I tossed at her side, staring at the ceiling in lonesome agony while she slept.

She slept not caring, not able to understand how I loved her, how I wanted to calm her night torments, how I wanted her to be the person I needed. The two of us a couple, I know now I was delusional. It didn't happen then, it hasn't happened now, and it will never happen in our future because that, thank anybody's creator, has ended. She was the person she was, period, take it or leave it.

I awoke on gray mornings, quiet, subdued, wondering what the dawn could bring. She noticed when I was quiet, and I could be quiet. I never thought of myself as quiet. In fact, I wasn't quiet, only when she destroyed my sense of self in such a thorough way that I was stunned.

Like a dazed animal I stood, legs splayed, eyes wide and rolling, while this jungle cat of a woman pulled out my guts. I looked for strength, which I knew I had, and instead found claws penetrating my throbbing heart.

Quiet I could be and still. I protected

myself by stillness, like the hiding fawn, the unmoving rabbit, the crouching grouse. When under the gaze of the hawk, the leopard in dark, not moving was one of my securities with her.

When I did make a run for it into the open, she knew it. I sang loud, rowdy songs, played my guitar while romancing my violin. I danced, and jumped, she purred, loving me for it. Loved it the way a barn cat watches a sparrow before it ends its life then eats it.

I wanted to think she was different inside than what I saw outside and there, wrapped up in plain sight, was the enigma. The human spirit is a camouflage. The eyes, the so-called windows to the soul, indeed can be windows, and just as often, masks. Like the skin of the chameleon, they can show what we want them to show. For some people the eyes are automatic in their rejection.

Judith's eyes were egg white, milk blue, a startling color. The color of the cast eye of the Australian shepherd. Small blue iridescent, opalescent flecks dotted her right eye and backlit the black of her pupil. Everyone mentioned Judith's eyes.

"I can see in the dark, don't worry," she told me once as she led me by the hand, not stumbling into a pine sage forest on abysmal, rainy night in Montana on a road trip.

Discordant thunder rolled through Lolo Pass, and near constant fork lighting made her eyes gleam. She walked deep, straight into the dark sobbing pines while the clashing lighting gave a nightmarish gray white to a surreal scene.

A flash and a buck deer, half of his antlers gone, stood in the blasted galvanized light. With each flash the buck walked as in a light show toward us, his movements jerky and bizarre. Judith squeezed my hand to stop, and then she walked toward the electric lit deer, her hand out, alone. She circled around the deer, and the deer circled around her. When Judith leaped, the deer leaped. They stared at one another in the rain, blackness, and jagged, fire-bolt blasts of silver white. The smell of sulfurous smoke, mountain sage, pine, damp moss, and lighting was in the air. They stood, gazing at each other in the flashes of light that showed fallen logs, moss, ferns, burnt stumps, and instantly a great white owl flew in and then out of the scene. The sky grew dark once again, and when the lighting flashed again, Judith, luminous, acid green, lit, was running to-ward me. Mad opal eyes, her hair, sopping wet, was plastered to her face. She came to me, singing, calling, chortling, pulling me down with the driving rain, while butcher-ing off my skin of wet clothes, leaving me naked on the floor of the forest. She stood, straddling me, ripping out her buttons, tearing her red shirt, soaked pants, and red underpants off in one intense blur. Poised high above me, her whiteness silhouetted by forking lighting flashes against the dark forest, her nipples erect, she fell on me, cold, slippery, and wet, like a spawning salmon. Her eyes gleaming iridescent. Me, white, scared, erect. She fell, covering me where I lay, with the exploding night rolling over us like a snow-gutted wave.

I awoke to frogs joyously, outrageously singing with the purling, babbling sound of water trickling through mossy rocks. Reflections of a full moon were on the surface of a small quiet pool by my side. Across the soft, moss lined stream, struck by moonbeams, the buck lay quietly, staring at Judith who sat by my side wrapped in my old green wool military coat, whistling softly at the buck.

Did we love each other, someone once asked. From my perspective, it was a moot question. I can't say about her, how could I?

And most of the time I couldn't say about me, but I know I loved her in the mountains. However, I could love anyone in those mountains. Give me a moment any day, give me a moment any year, jumble them all together, and I am still in love.

Twisted arrows of dead trees silhouetted against dark pine forests, canyons turned down and fell to plunging, raging white water, wet as sex and more urgent. I lived to breathe this. Gnarled streams through moss velvet stones, red willow, skunk cabbage, cobwebs levitating on motes of distant sun, aspens quaking and rich as sauternes. My heart runs to love.

To be near naked freshets of snow melt and golden trout under gray-pink staggering cliffs, setting sun the color of watermelon left magic in my body like returning salmon.

Driving her tiny open car through mountain slashed canyons of grunting elk,

Judith took off her clothes and covered herself with my old World War I officer's coat. She leaned, warm, bare skinned, bare breasted, tender, and sumptuous against my arms, her hands kneading my chest and flushed neck. The scent of deep river shady groves, smelling freshly of skunk and trout, rushed in and around us in her fragile little open car. High mountain passes, secluded and summer snowcapped, came and went, the frigid air nipping and searing, top down, heater on full, Judith's lips ticking like a moist clock in my ear. She forgot that I was driving. Her large sucking lips were on my face, my arms, hands pulling at my belt, my zipper, waist, shirt, grinding lips on my under belly until the chaos of thinking, feeling, and driving made my feet contract from the pedals. Moaning, I choked on velvet emotion, went blind to my existence, opened my passion filled eyes, and saw bridge abutments coming at me. I felt my death as cars and horns blared at my erratic course through moss and mist filled river bottoms. I searched the winding road ahead for places to stop, logging roads, long driveways, jerking and quivering, my jellied passions hardly controlled, barely missing on-coming cars. I found a spot beside a field. Groping, refusing to let go of her erect hold on me, Judith rushed us over barbwire fences, sprawling into cropped grasses on the other side of a small knolls, just off the roadway. We fell and spawned to primal passions. She gave and I came again and again under reefs of astral galaxies, crying for the joy of thrusting purling waters.

Waking, in unmeasured time, feet in cold wetness, our bodies buried for warmth under tangles of clothes, our silver spawning spent, we shivered, standing naked, dressing under a thousand kind of stars. Cows champing dewy night grasses watched silently as we giggled, kissing again and again, walking the barbed fence in search of our abandoned car.

Once as we stood peering into the Snake River Canyon a mood took me, and for a moment, as in those moments in sleep, I saw myself falling deeply, sharply down, and following my inward eye as I fell, I saw at the canyon bottom a lone horseback rider beside a remote and gentle river. My mood changed to one of hundreds of years ago. I was alive with unknowns. I had a good horse under me following ancient trade routes, longing in wolf-like glances up birch scattered valleys, fearing the Blackfoot and the Sioux.

Seeing the moon rise in mute, splendid beauty in the ripples of the river, months from love, howling in fire, God laughter, in deep thought beneath hides as sleep showed me me. Judith looked at me and said my eyes scared her.

We arrived at Overland Pipe's the next

day in the early afternoon. His home was a log cabin made from enormous logs. It was situated on a bend on the upper Yellow Stone overlooking distant snow-capped peaks.

"Come in, come in," he chortled pleasantly. "Looks like you two could use a drink. How about a beer?" Then as an afterthought he said, "And an aquavit chaser that would, of course, be jubulayams, since the two of you look so jubilant."

Then he laughed his warm, chuckling laugh. Judith looked over at him, saying nothing. She wasn't threatened by anyone, however, Overland definitely took some thought.

The beer on an empty stomach was refreshing and the aquavit was a lifesaver.

Judith and me had spent the morning sitting in bed in the log cabin motel in front of the fireplace talking of good times. When she was happy, she was my joy, but I could never think for a moment that I really knew what she was going to do next. I didn't. For me, she was a grenade with the pin pulled.

Overland looked over at her quietly. People of learning, sensitive types, those with curiosity, could tell Judith was educated, moneyed, eccentric, and traveled. Judith spoke five languages fluently and understood smatterings of scores of others. Menu language, she called it. Judith brought much to the game and took as much away.

Neither Judith nor Overland said more than a simple hello, while I tried to talk it up to fill the pregnant silence, which became a non-fruit bearing experience.

Judith had the quality of extreme silence when she wished, to the point of completely ignoring someone, even if asked a direct question. You can guess the effect of that on many people she met—bitch!

Overland asked her nothing. Somehow, he knew her answers would be non-starters. He was in his house, on his land, he was secure.

His house, while not overly huge, was made of big logs and beams in grandiose proportion. The fireplace was of multicolored conglomerate river stones and would probably have held Runner. Six-foot logs were smoldering and looked as if they had been burning since the night before. Large windows filled with mineral blue Montana sky notched the walls. The atmosphere in the room was slightly smoky and warm, warm enough that I became sleepy.

I sat quietly, a refilled aquavit in my hand, an ice-cold Coors on my side table, listening to the occasional pop of the logs. At times, lost to my thoughts, I jumped when the logs popped.

A large Eustace Ziegler painting of Mount McKinley dominated the large log mantel.

Tibetan prayer rugs carpeted the polished wood floors near a small camp or wood shrine. The shrine held a bronze of the Blood Goddess Cali.

On another wall was a long vertical painting of a monk's room in a temple, a serene scene. The room, the whole house for that matter, was an art gallery.

Another painting showed a clown dressed in black with white vertical stripes seated at a lime green dressing table. His make-up jars on the table and a mirror to his side showing his clownish haunted profile. Nothing was funny.

Overland and Judith were alike. I could see it in the many ways they each had. The way they acted, the way their homes were arranged, laid out and cluttered.

The unique artwork, the Zen-God quality of various fine art, articles of sculpture, porcelain, etchings, etc., and the mad house arrangement of this disparate assortment.

They were both transcendent, they were

international. Their world was just that, their world. They controlled the world and the atmosphere around them. Even more, they were a law unto themselves. Mountainous, isolated, high human peaks rising majestically over the lowland peasants.

And people like me? Detritus ground fine!

Grains of grey, finely pulverized sand, empty hearts, ice crystals in hollow chambers that pulse and throb in fear. There was that fear of love, and do I really need to say it, fear of rejection. What did Housman say?

"And while the sun and moon endure, luck's a chance, but trouble's sure." Be happy, be guarded, not for me!

Who wants to be guarded in love? But then after nights of loveless intercourse, I could never call it lovemaking, only screwing. What else could I call those frigid events in her bed, in her little floating boathouse in Seattle?

I dragged on my wrinkled cold clothes in the streetlights, stabbing through eerie dark at the side of her bedroom window while she, sexually fulfilled, blissfully slept, unaware I was alive. I was her stud and she treated me that way.

In anguish and confusion, I zipped up my pants once more and stumbled up her rain slick boathouse dock, finding my way through soaking rains to the cold steel blob that would be my sopping, dripping wet car. Sometimes I drove away, in fact though, I rarely did drive away. Why? I don't know, maybe you know. Or maybe I did know but wouldn't say it. The world is not an easy place for those who fall in love and are rejected. Confusion reigns.

The question is when to start to protect yourself in that rejected situation, then, of course, when to stop protecting yourself, so as not to jeopardize what you hope will be love in return. Then next, how to advance to love when you feel ignored and somehow know, even then, early, that it will alway be that way. Can you believe her, or have events really swung out of your favor? Are you no longer favored? How can that be after all that was said?

But then when you told her you loved her, she said,

"Stick it." When you said,

"I love you," she said,

"Die."

When I said all, I wanted was to be near her she said,

"Piss on you."

That's pretty clear, isn't it? But I didn't want to believe it. You know this one, so pathetic, but I thought I could change her. Even in those days, I refused to believe what I knew inwardly was a fact: She didn't love me and more, she was incapable of intimate love.

I knew I was special, or at least I thought

I was special. Wasn't I?

Sitting behind the steering wheel in that damp, cold car on the night's street, passing cars were distorted, wet hissing blobs of glaring white headlights and blurry red taillights.

I always got caught waiting. Judith made me wait. Judith didn't make me wait, I waited, I admit it, she dazzled me.

Sometimes, my car running, the radio playing, the windows completely fogged up, I wrapped myself in my old military WWI coat.

I dozed, sleepless, my forehead mashed on the cold plastic steering wheel. I was hunched over like an old man trying to piss.

I waited, sometimes for hours. Sometimes I forgot I was waiting when the door would suddenly wrench open. Judith, in her drenched pajamas, barefoot, standing in a leadened downpour, wet and disheveled, mad and pleading, I never knew which, would start to pound on me with her fists.

Her cruel voice was a harsh sound out of a discordant nightmare. Jagged gray mercury vapor lights glared off of her frantic face. God, her face in that light scared me. Me, wet and cold, she, screaming, neighbors started turning on porch lights.

She, heavy with late night sleeplessness, maddened with emotion, angry kinds of rain pasted every airy thing to her body like a wet sock. Her hair a warlock's druid, her skin the color of Melville's hideous whale.

Her face was the translucence of the white underbelly of the shark, the color of death, destructive mayhem.

When she screamed at me like this, the engorged red blood vessels were frighteningly visible just beneath the surface of her forehead. She never held anything back. I don't think she could have.

"Let me in, oh God, let me in that God

damn car! How could you leave me sleeping in that inky black room alone?"

Dogs barked, her voice a torn wet rag soaked by night rains. In the car, straddling me in a cold wet embrace, pulling at my belt and zipper, her urgency exciting me, she moaned into the darkened ceiling of the car, scratching claw-like at my head as she raised her wet pajamas and settled against my warmth. Her needs were desperate, she confused me always.

In love, like politics, nobody knows anything. We stumble and fall, get up if we are lucky and try again. And if by some miracle something works, it is really only a small part of a greater mystery that few can define.

Two people standing in their own tower of Babel like separate observers at an accident, each with a nanosecond to make a guess as to what happened. Should I entrust my life to this person, or should I run away?

"Whatever is reality today, whatever you touch and believe in and that seems real for you today, is going to be - like the reality of yesterday - an illusion tomorrow."

We always belong to the power we choose to obey!

"Love! In what folly do you not contrive to make us find pleasure?"

Is that why vigorous lovemaking sounds like gasping and dying, what my French friend calls the climax, the little death?

This is the world some of us live in.

It is the world of which we are a part of, like it or not. We are cosmic hamburger; our importance is overrated, except how you can make a positive difference for your kind and your planet.

Within each of us, like some great geologic, fleshy conglomerate, there are encapsulated wounds and joys. These joys and wounds are sometimes visible, sometime not. After all, we know people who hide their emotions, their wounds, very well. For some unknown reason, people also hide their joys.

No one, however craftily they may try, can hide their wounds and joys all the time. There are births, deaths, romances, successes, failures, and despair.

Here, in this spot above my heart, perhaps there is pain from some rejection. Right at the middle back of my cervical spine there is a reminder that one dark snowy night a man forgot to stop behind my car with his car and now my neck has hurt forever. By my lower right rib, maybe the feeling of joy from my first kiss. Maybe inside my right knee there is pain from a long-ago skiing accident. My knee remembers. Your knee can think.

Possibly there is a painful stricken shoulder from a now long-dead romance.

Perhaps there is that great sensual glowing in your thighs thinking of last night. These distant, miserable, and joyful events affect us in ways we feel but no longer remember, but our bodies remember. Where does the body hide the pain when the pain isn't manifesting?

The history of our bodies is a study of our fortunes and misfortunes, plainly visible to those who care and have the talent to detect and understand. Your breathing, your sighs, your screams in the night, your moans, your agony in love, your agony in pain, it's all there.

It is tattooed inside and outside our lovely bodies by our experiences.

Suffer and hate too much, you may destroy your lungs. Love to much, you become unguarded. What then?

Your arms, your beautiful, rounded arms, still remember last night's embrace.

Muscles have memory. "Memory is

more indelible than ink."

We are not igneous, we are metamorphic. Metamorphic rock arises from the transformation of existing rock to new types of rock through transformative events. When two chemicals react to each other they are forever changed. Most emotional scars show, yet many don't. Don't show for years, decades, until, like a stealth saboteur, they arrive from deep inside of us, throw a sabot into the gears of our brains, and we wake up crying, wondering why.

In our vulnerabilities, through pain and suffering, love and hate, despair and joy, we become completely transformed from the innocent child we were that issued from our mother's womb.

Many scars remain apparent, a few occasionally disappear from sight but remain inside of us. The joy of a new day, the wrinkled brow, the bitten nail, the sob at night.

"The past grows gradually around us,

like a placenta dying."

One day, sitting on a log on the beach down in the redwood country of northern California, I idly wrote Judith's name with a piece of crooked silver driftwood in the wet sand.

My etching was beside a small gentle swelling of tidal water where it made a little advancing creek at each gentle wave from the sea. It washed in, then softly washed out.

As I stood up, watching the soft, ever so gentle waves, they gradually, so insistently caved, then crumbled the sharply etched letters of her name to simple, meaningless calligraphy. Small peaceful wave after sunlit wave rolled in, then out, and soon it was as though her name had never been written in the smooth sand at all. Even more than this, it was as if she never existed.

"Alas, our frailty is the cause, not we, for such as we are made of, such we be."

To author and artist Douglas Granum, creation is a way of life.

His inspiration is derived from his travels around the world and an appreciation of the unusual — trekking the jungles of New Guinea, enjoying plein aire painting in northern Urals of Russia, drifting down China's Yangtze River, looking at the stars in a Serengeti night sky, and commercial fishing in the storm-tossed Gulf of Alaska.

As an artist Douglas Granum works with and in various mediums including stone, metal, glass, wood, canvas, bronze and of course, writing. From creation in his studio in Southworth, Washington, his paintings, glass pieces, metal and stone sculptures can be found worldwide.

Find out more at DouglasGranum.com

Other stories by Douglas Granum:

THE ROSE COVERED COTTAGE

THE GERMAN MUSIC TEACHER'S COTTAGE

ALONE ON THE YELLOWSTONE

WAR NO PEACE (PARTS I, II)

FRANKIE LE BOUCHON

DEATH AND AFTERLIFE ON EL PASEO

Find out more at DouglasGranum.com